Can You Tell the Difference?

Is It an Alligator or a Crocodile?

Gail Terp

BLACK RABBIT BOOKS

Hi Jinx is published by Black Rabbit Books
P.O. Box 227, Mankato, Minnesota, 56002.
www.blackrabbitbooks.com

Marysa Storm, editor; Michael Sellner, designer;
Omay Ayres, photo researcher

Library of Congress
Cataloging-in-Publication Data
Names: Terp, Gail, 1951- author.
Title: Is it an alligator or a crocodile? / by Gail Terp.
Description: Mankato, Minnesota : Black Rabbit Books, [2020] | Series: Hi jinx. Can you tell the difference? | Audience: Age 9-12. | Audience: Grade 4 to 6. | Includes bibliographical references and index.
Identifiers: LCCN 2018023341 (print) | LCCN 2018025485 (ebook) | ISBN 9781680729085 (e-book) | ISBN 9781680729023 (library binding) | ISBN 9781644660560(paperback)
Subjects: LCSH: Alligators–Juvenile literature. | Crocodiles–Juvenile literature.
Classification: LCC QL666.C925 (ebook) | LCC QL666.C925 T47 2020 (print) | DDC 597.98/4-dc23
LC record available at https://lccn.loc.gov/2018023341

Image Credits

Alamy: RooM the Agency, 15 (btm); Julio Carmelo Fuentes, 19 (A); Media Drum World, 20 (btm); Timothy Large, 15; iStock: carlosalvarez, Cover; Shutterstock: AFMARCOS, 19 (C); Aluna1, 6–7 (bkgd); Anan Kaewkhammul, 1; Arto Hakola, 11 (top); benchart, Cover (sky, clouds); Christos Georghiou, 23 (btm torn paper); David Grigg, 4–5 (bkgd); doddis77, Cover (bubble), 1 (bubble), 19 (bubble); Dualororua, 18 (right croc); ekler, 14 (torn paper); Filipe Frazao, 23 (croc); GraphicsRF, 18 (signs); Heiko Kiera, 14 (gator), 19 (B); HitToon, 21 (croc); Julien Tromeur, Cover (left croc); Khvost, Cover (grass); lazy clouds, 8–9 (map); Memo Angeles, 4 (girl), 6, 6–7 (fish), 7, 12 (croc); new photo, 11 (btm); Oleksandr Desiatkin, Back Cover (bkgd), 3, 11 (bkgd), 21 (bkgd); opicobello, 12 (torn corner); Pasko Maksim, Back Cover (torn edge), 16, 23 (top), 24; pitju, 9 (curl), 17, 21 (curl); Rafal Lukasik, 1; Refluo, 4–5 (mosquitoes); Rohit Dhanaji Shinde, 2–3, 8; Ron Dale, 5, 8 (marker stroke), 18 (marker stroke), 20 (top); Sergey Uryadnikov, 6–7 (croc), 16–17; Sujono sujono, 18 (left croc); Susan Flashman, 12–13 (croc); totallypic, 13; worldswildlifewonders, 19 (D); your, 12–13 (clouds) Every effort has been made to contact copyright holders for material reproduced in this book. Any omissions will be rectified in subsequent printings if notice is given to the publisher.

Contents

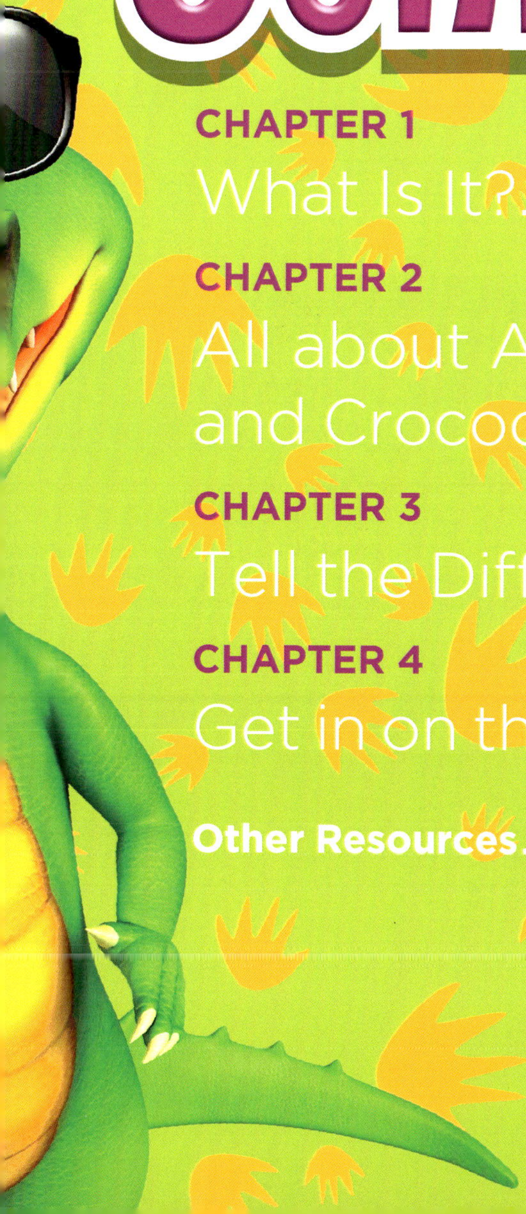

Chapter 1
What Is It?

It's a hot summer day in the Florida **Everglades**. You're surrounded by **lush** plants, swampy water, and *tons* of mosquitoes. Suddenly, something begins swimming toward you. You can only see the top of its scaly head. It's an alligator. No, it's a crocodile. Ack! Which scary **reptile** is it?

A Lot Alike

It's a good thing you're about to learn about gators and crocs. You never know when you might run into one. These two animals have a lot in common. They can be difficult to tell apart. They're both reptiles, and they both have murderous teeth. But this guide can help you tell the difference. That way, you'll know which animal is trying to eat you!

Chapter 2

All about Alligators and Crocodiles

Alligators and crocodiles look alike, but they do have many differences. For starters, they usually live in different places. Alligators only live in the southeastern United States and part of China. Crocs live around the world, except where it is very cold. So don't go looking for them in Antarctica!

Where They Live

Alligators prefer fresh water. But crocodiles aren't so picky. They live in both fresh water and salt water. Crocs can live in both types of water because they have salt **glands**. After they swallow salty water, the glands push the salt out.

It's All in the Snout

Looking at the **snouts** is an easy way to tell the difference. Wide, U-shaped snouts belong to gators. Crocodiles have narrow, V-shaped snouts.

The teeth are another good clue. When gators close their mouths, their super sharp bottom teeth are hidden. When crocs close their mouths, you can still see their lower teeth.

Crocs have up to 68 terrifying teeth. Imagine how long it'd take to brush them all!

alligator

crocodile

The Chinese crocodile only grows up to 5 feet (1.5 meters) long.

Oh My, They're Big!

All alligators and crocodiles might seem huge. But gators are actually smaller. The American alligator grows up to 15 feet (4.5 m) long. But saltwater crocodiles can easily reach more than 20 feet (6 m) long. You'd fit in their big bodies pretty easily!

Color Coded

Gators and crocs tend to be colored differently. Gators are darker. They're often a blackish gray or brown. Crocs are lighter and can be gray-green or light brown. The color really makes their hungry eyes stand out. Don't you think?

Baby alligators have yellow stripes. The stripes help camouflage the little reptiles.

alligator

crocodile

Crocodile attacks are more common than shark attacks.

Danger!

Crocodiles are usually more **aggressive** than alligators. They're more likely to pick fights and attack. Saltwater and Nile crocodiles are the most dangerous crocs. They'll eat anything and everything, including people. Gators are shy. They'll only attack if hungry or scared. But they usually **avoid** people.

Chapter 3
Tell the Difference

At first glance, crocodiles and alligators might look the same. But now you know their differences.

A

B

Is It an ALLigator or a CrocodiLe?

C

D

Answers on page 21.

Chapter 4

Get in on the HiJinx

You're not the only one who likes these animals. Researchers like them too. And they've discovered a really cool thing. Gators and crocs like to play! They surf on waves and splash in water. At times, crocs play with other crocs, giving piggyback rides. Gators play with one another too. Maybe you have more in common with them than you thought!

Take It One Step More

1. Crocodiles and alligators have different snout shapes. Why do you think that is? Do some research to find out.

2. Why do alligators avoid swimming in salt water?

3. Make a **Venn diagram** using alligator and crocodile features. Do you think they are more alike or different?

A. crocodile B. alligator
C. alligator D. crocodile

GLOSSARY

aggressive (uh-GRES-iv)—showing a readiness to fight, argue, or attack

avoid (uh-VOYD)—to keep away from

camouflage (KA-muh-flazh)—something, such as color or shape, that protects an animal from attack by making the animal difficult to see in the area around it

Everglades (EV-er-gleydz)—a large swamp region of southern Florida

gland (GLAND)—a body part that produces a substance to be used by the body or given off from it

lush (LUHSH)—covered with healthy green plants

reptile (REP-tile)—a cold-blooded animal that breathes air and has a backbone; most reptiles lay eggs and have scaly skin.

snout (SNOUT)—the projecting part of an animal's face that includes the nose or nose and mouth

Venn diagram (VEN DAHY-uh-gram)—a diagram that shows the relationship between two groups of things by means of overlapping circles

LEARN MORE

BOOKS

Alligator. My Favorite Animal. Ann Arbor, MI: Cherry Lake Publishing, 2018.

Gish, Ashley. *Crocodiles.* Reptiles. Mankato, MN: Creative Education, 2019.

Ryndak, Rob. *Alligator or Crocodile?* Animal Look-Alikes. New York: Gareth Stevens Publishing, 2016.

WEBSITES

American Alligator
nationalzoo.si.edu/animals/american-alligator

American Crocodiles
video.nationalgeographic.com/video/croc_american

Nile Crocodile
kids.nationalgeographic.com/animals/nile-crocodile/#crocodile-teeth.png

INDEX